Sleep Softly

Classical Lullabies by Brahms, Schubert, Satie, Debussy...

Performed by L'Ensemble Agora
Illustrated by Élodie Nouhen

1 Barcarolle

Excerpt from The Tales of Hoffmann (Act 3)
Jacques Offenbach

Barcarolles are folk songs of the Venetian gondoliers characterized by a gentle ternary rhythm that suggests the rocking of a boat. Jacques Offenbach composed this one for his opera *The Tales of Hoffmann*, first performed at the Opéra-Comique in 1881. Although the work was not completed before the composer died in October 1880, it would go on to establish his international reputation. Inspired by the life and stories of the German writer E.T.A. Hoffmann, the opera recounts the tragic love story of a poet.

Act 3 takes place in Venice, where Hoffmann—despite renouncing love in favour of a life of carousing and pleasure—is seduced by the courtesan Giulietta, who steals his reflection in a magic mirror.

The act opens with this famous barcarolle, whose haunting rhythm and memorable melody invite Hoffmann and the listener to allow themselves to be seduced by the pleasures of Venice. The gentle music is deceptive, for it is intended to mask a diabolical plot threatening Hoffmann's very soul!

2 Après un rêve (After a Dream)

Gabriel Fauré

Composed in 1878, this famous melody is probably Gabriel Fauré's most familiar work. The original version for voice is set to verse by Romain Bussine (1830–1899) modelled on Tuscan poetry, but the music has been transcribed for many different instruments, including the cello, saxophone and even trombone. The orchestration of the recording introduces the melody in the bass clarinet, whose gentle, melancholic timbre suits the dreamlike atmosphere of the poem perfectly.

After a Dream epitomizes Fauré's style: a simple melody combined with the composer's original harmonies creates a charming otherworldly quality.

In a slumber which held your image spellbound
I dreamt of happiness, passionate mirage
Your eyes were softer, your voice pure and sonorous
You shone like a sky lit up by the dawn

You called me and I left the earth
To run away with you towards the light
The skies opened their clouds for us
Unknown splendours, divine flashes glimpsed

Alas! Alas! sad awakening from dreams
I call you, O night, give me back your lies
Return, return radiant
Return, O mysterious night

3 Von Fremden Ländern
(Of Foreign Lands)

Excerpt from *Kinderszenen – Scenes from Childhood*
Robert Schumann

Scenes from Childhood is a cycle of thirteen short piano pieces. Robert Schumann himself confessed that they were written by an overgrown child. He composed the work in 1838 during an unhappy period in his life: the father of Clara, his long-time love, had refused to permit them to marry. As a victim of social customs impeding the fulfillment of his love, was Schumann perhaps drawn back nostalgically to memories of childhood—that innocent world where dreams are realized, where a rocking horse is a proud stallion, where a name on a map evokes a foreign land?

In the version on the CD, the music ebbs and flows through the crystal-clear sound of the harp. Other instruments gradually come and go, as though a music box was inviting one to dream.

4 La Boîte à joujoux (The Toybox)
Claude Debussy

The Toybox was originally composed for the piano in 1913, based on a children's book by André Hellé (1871–1945). Claude Debussy later orchestrated the work to accompany a puppet show. As the third scene opens, war is over, and the little soldier can finally rest with his wife, the Doll, in their new home. In the distance, a shepherd plays this air accompanied only by echoes from the mountain.

The English horn orchestration of the melody is reminiscent of the solo from Act 3 of Wagner's *Tristan and Isolde*, an opera admired by Debussy. However, the clarity of his pentatonic melody is quite different from the sombre, tormented character of Wagner's music.

A pentatonic melody is one that can be played on the black keys of a piano. This means that it is restricted to just five consonant notes, lending the music a floating quality that recalls certain styles of Asian music.

5 Gymnopédie No. 1

Erik Satie

The Gymnopedia was a religious festival in honour of Apollo, at which young Spartan men danced naked. Satie envisaged this dancing as a kind of waltz to a slow, heavy rhythm that is appropriate to the ritualistic nature of the event and also evokes the scorching heat of July, when the festival was held.

Satie chose to compose light, unpretentious music in stark contrast to the monumental works of Wagner and Mahler that were in vogue at the time he was writing. In 1917, he began referring to his compositions as furniture music: easy to listen to, but not intended for the serious context of a concert hall. Despite the reduced—almost minimalist—intention of *Gymnopédie No. 1*, which was composed in 1888, the work has a special charm that clearly makes it more than simple background music! This charm comes from the harmonic finesse that Satie, like Debussy, learned from Fauré.

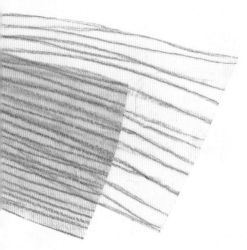

6 La Poupée (The Doll)

Excerpt from *Jeux d'enfants* (*Children's Games*)
Georges Bizet

Georges Bizet composed *Children's Games,* a series of twelve piano pieces for four hands, a few months before the birth of his son Jacques. Childhood was a source of inspiration for many Romantic composers, including Robert Schumann (*Scenes from Childhood*), Camille Saint-Saëns (*Carnival of the Animals*) and Francis Poulenc (*The Story of Babar the Little Elephant*). Despite being light and simple, these works for children fully express the artistic mastery of their composers. This is particularly true in the case of *The Doll*, a sublimely delicate work that Bizet later orchestrated in his *Petite Suite*, under the title *Berceuse*.

A piece for piano four hands is played by two pianists at the same instrument—a genre particularly well-suited to pedagogical works. Bizet probably intended to introduce his son to the piano by playing *Children's Games* with him. Unfortunately, he never had the opportunity as he died in 1875 when Jacques was only three.

7 Sandmännchen (The Little Sandman)

Excerpt from *15 Volkskinderlieder – 15 Children's Folk Songs*
Johannes Brahms

When Clara and Robert Schumann met Johannes Brahms for the first time in 1853, they were immediately struck by the genius of the twenty-year-old pianist. Robert responded with enthusiastic reviews for the musical press, while Clara included some of Brahms' early piano pieces in her concert repertoire. Following Robert's tragic death in 1856, Brahms remained close to Clara, and so it was only natural that he dedicate to the Schumann children the collection of popular songs that includes this lullaby.

On the CD, the melody is distributed among several instruments, a truly original orchestration. While the work is quite recognizable, it constantly changes colour like a prism whose reflections vary as the viewer holds it at different angles. Known as tone-colour melody (from the German *Klangfarbenmelodie*), this technique was originally used by Hector Berlioz in the first half of the 19th century and then further developed at the beginning of the 20th century, primarily by Arnold Schoenberg (who coined the term) and by Anton Webern.

Die Blümelein, sie schlafen	*The flowers are long asleep*
Schon längst im Mondenschein	*In the moonlight*
Sie nicken mit den Köpfen	*They nod their heads*
Auf ihren Stengelein	*On slender stems*
Es rüttelt sich der Blütenbaum	*The blossoming tree's a-quiver*
Er säuselt wie im Traum	*Whispering as in a dream*
Schlafe, schlafe, schlaf du, mein Kindelein	*Sleep, sleep, my child*

8 Wiegenlied (Lullaby)

Johannes Brahms

Who has not experienced being rocked to sleep as a baby by the sound of a music box playing this tune? It is a *lied* composed by Johannes Brahms in 1868. The first verse is taken from *Des Knaben Wunderhorn* (*The Boy's Magic Horn*), a collection of popular German songs published between 1805 and 1808. The same collection also inspired a song cycle by Gustav Mahler.

The melody is well known, but the orchestration on the CD emphasizes the subtle counterpoint of the accompaniment. For example, as the oboe plays the main melody, a flute motive can be heard sparkling above.

Lied (plural *lieder*) is the German word for melody and refers to a solo song with piano accompaniment. The term is often used to distinguish the songs of Schubert, Brahms, Mahler and Strauss from French art song, which has quite a different style.

Counterpoint is the technique of superimposing several melodic lines such that they complement one another. The undisputed master of counterpoint was Johann Sebastian Bach, who was a powerful influence on many 19th-century German composers, including Brahms.

Guten Abend, gute Nacht	*Good evening, good night*
Mit Rosen bedacht	*With roses covered*
Mit Näglein besteckt	*With carnations adorned*
Schlupf unter die Deck	*Slip under the covers*
Morgen früh, wenns Gott will	*Tomorrow morning, if God wants so*
Wirst du wieder geweckt	*You will wake once again*
Guten Abend, gute Nacht	*Good evening, good night*
Von Englein bewacht	*By angels watched*
Die zeigen im Traum	*Who show you in your dream*
Dir Christkindleins Baum	*The Christ-child's tree*
Schlaf nun selig und süß	*Sleep now blissfully and sweetly*
Schau im Traum's Paradies	*See paradise in your dreams*

9 Solveig's Song

Excerpt from *Peer Gynt*

Edvard Grieg

In 1875, Edvard Grieg composed incidental music for *Peer Gynt* by Norwegian playwright Henrik Ibsen. Peer Gynt is the work's slightly mad hero who abandons Solveig to wander the world in a desperate search for his identity. When he returns to Norway old, tired and dissatisfied, Solveig—who has always remained true—awaits and greets him with this song.

The song is in two distinct sections. The first, which comes back in at the end, is a sombre Slavic-style melody in a minor key expressing the dismay of abandonment. By contrast, the lighter second section in a major key suggests that, despite everything, Solveig has remained firm in her belief that Peer Gynt would would eventually return.

Kanske vil der gå både Vinter og vår
Og næste Sommer med, og det hele år
Men engang vil du komme, det véd jeg visst
Og jeg skal nok vente, for det lovte jeg sidst

Gud styrke dig, hvor du i Verden går
Gud glæde dig, hvis du for hans Fodskammel står
Her skal jeg vente til du kommer igen
Og venter du histoppe, vi træffes der, min Ven

The winter may go, and the spring disappear
Next summer, too, may fade, and the whole long year
But you will be returning, in truth, I know
And I will wait for you as I promised long ago

May God guide and keep you, wherever you may go
Upon you His blessing and mercy bestow
And here I will await you till you are here
And if you are in Heaven, I'll meet you there

10 Schlafe, mein Prinzchen, schlaf ein

(Sleep, My Little Prince, Fall Asleep)

Bernhard Flies

For a long time, this lullaby was erroneously attributed to Wolfgang Amadeus Mozart. Instead, Bernhard Flies, a German physician and amateur composer, composed it in 1799. The text comes from the play *Esther* by Friedrich Wilhelm Gotter.

Like many lullabies, this one features a ternary rhythm which may suggest either the movement of a mother rocking her child or a spinning Viennese waltz. This ambiguity is reinforced by the stylized accompaniment to the melody. On the CD, the orchestration calls to mind the sound of an organ-grinder.

Schlafe, mein Prinzchen, schlaf ein	*Sleep, my little prince, fall asleep*
Es ruhn Schäfchen und Vögelein	*The lambs and birdies are resting*
Garten und Wiese verstummt	*The garden and meadow are silent*
Auch nicht ein Bienchen mehr summt	*And even the little bee hums no more*
Luna mit silbernem Schein	*Luna with a silver gleam*
Gucket zum Fenster herein	*Is pouring her light into the window*
Schlafe beim silbernen Schein	*Sleep by the silvery light*
Schlafe, mein Prinzchen, schlaf ein	*Sleep, my little prince, fall asleep*

11 Ständchen (Serenade)

Excerpt from *Schwanengesang – Swan Song*
Franz Schubert

According to Greek legend, a swan releases a final sublimely melodic song as it approaches death. When Franz Schubert's last song cycle appeared a few months after the composer's death in 1828, his publisher named the collection *Swan Song* as a musical testament to the late composer.

On the CD, the melody is repeated three times with slight variations. The third time, for example, the harp answers the oboe as though it were an echo. It's an idea borrowed from Franz Liszt, who transcribed Schubert's *Serenade* for solo piano.

Ever since the Middle Ages, serenades have been sung at night below a lady's window for the purpose of winning her heart. In Ludwig Rellstab's poem set by Schubert, the moon, the nightingales and all of nature join voices to plead the poet's love.

Leise flehen meine Lieder	*My songs beckon softly*
Durch die Nacht zu dir	*Through the night to you*
In den stillen Hain hernieder	*Below in the quiet grove*
Liebchen, komm zu mir	*Come to me, beloved*
Flüsternd schlanke Wipfel rauschen	*The rustle of slender leaf tips whispers*
In des Mondes Licht	*In the moonlight*
Des Verräters feindlich Lauschen	*Do not fear the evil spying*
Fürchte, Holde, nicht	*Of the betrayer, my dear*
Hörst die Nachtigallen schlagen?	*Do you hear the nightingales call?*
Ach! sie flehen dich	*Ah, they beckon to you*
Mit der Töne süßen Klagen	*With the sweet sound of their singing*
Flehen sie für mich	*They beckon to you for me*

12 Gute nacht (Good Night)

Excerpt from *Winterreise(Winter Journey)*
Franz Schubert

Winterreise is a well-known song cycle composed in 1827 to poems by Wilhelm Müller. It describes the wanderings of a traveller whose solitude is reflected in the sombre cold of the wintry landscape. The work is an emblematic masterpiece of German Romanticism. In the first song, the traveller abandons his beloved in the middle of the night for having betrayed him, offering a simple but ironic "Good night" as he leaves.

Fremd bin ich eingezogen	*As a stranger I arrived*
Fremd zieh' ich wieder aus	*As a stranger again I leave*
Der Mai war mir gewogen	*May was kind to me*
Mit manchem Blumenstrauß	*With many bunches of flowers*
Das Mädchen sprach von Liebe	*The girl spoke of love*
Die Mutter gar von Eh'	*Her mother even of marriage*
Nun ist die Welt so trübe	*Now the world is bleak*
Der Weg gehüllt in Schnee	*The path covered by snow*
Will dich im Traum nicht stören	*I will not disturb you in your dreaming*
Wär schad' um deine Ruh'	*It would be a pity to disturb your rest*
Sollst meinen Tritt nicht hören	*You shall not hear my footsteps*
Sacht, sacht die Türe zu!	*Softly, softly shut the door!*
Schreib' im Vorübergehen	*On my way out I'll write*
Ans Tor dir: Gute Nacht	*"Good night" on the gate*
Damit du mögest sehen	*So that you may see*
An dich hab' ich gedacht	*That I have thought of you*

13 Pavane de la Belle au bois dormant

(Sleeping Beauty's Pavane)

Excerpt from *Ma mère l'Oye (Mother Goose)*
Maurice Ravel

Following in the footsteps of Georges Bizet, between 1908 and 1910 Maurice Ravel composed a suite of pieces for piano four hands dedicated to the children of friends, and then orchestrated them in 1911. Ravel took his inspiration from Charles Perrault's *Contes*, also known as *Contes de ma mère l'Oye* (*Tales of Mother Goose*).

For *Sleeping Beauty*, Ravel composed a pavane—a 16th-century dance that Gabriel Fauré had already borrowed. The slow, majestic pace of the music and the ancient sound of Ravel's harmonies take the listener straight within the tale's mysterious castle where time has been suspended for the last hundred years.

The origin of the word *pavane* is uncertain. It may refer to a dance from the town of Padua (in Italian, *pavano* means "from Padua"), or the word may derive from the Latin *pavo* for peacock. Whatever the origin, one thing is certain: in French *se pavaner* means to strut like a peacock!

14 Feuillet d'album (Album Leaf)

Excerpt from *Cinq Pièces posthumes* *(Five Posthumous Pieces)*
Emmanuel Chabrier

An album leaf is a short piece intended not for publication, but simply as a gift to another musician—in this case, to the pianist Édouard Risler. Composed in 1897, Chabrier's *Album Leaf* was part of a collection of five piano pieces that would be published after the composer's death. It provides an example of several influences that marked Chabrier's music. The arpeggios are reminiscent of Schumann, while certain harmonic subtleties derive from the Belgian-born composer César Franck. Certain chords may be arpeggiated rather than struck simultaneously. This technique offers the pianist a rich means of expression that was popular with Romantic composers.

15 Dors, ami (Sleep, My Friend)

Excerpt from *Don César de Bazan*
Jules Massenet

This lullaby is from Jules Massenet's opera *Don César de Bazan* (1872), based on a libretto by Adolphe d'Ennery. At the beginning of Act 2, Don César sleeps in his cell after being condemned to death for participating in a duel during Holy Week. The lullaby is sung to him by his friend, Lazarille. Unbeknownst to the audience, Lazarille owes his life to Don César and so has removed the bullets from the rifles to be used by the platoon to execute the prisoner.

This calm, peaceful melody is in sharp contrast to the frenetic tragedy that marks the conclusion to Act 1. Such dramatic juxtaposition between the end of one act and the start of the next was popular with nineteenth-century opera composers.

Sleep, my friend, sleep,
Bring thee sweet joys tho' only seeming
And rock thee to slumber deep
Sleep, my friend, O sleep, my only friend

It seems that while you're dreaming
The rays from rosy skies
In heaven brightly gleaming
Bless and caress your tired eyes

No! The pure light that's glowing
Upon your brow divine
Will surely not be going
But will again tomorrow shine!

16 Brezairola (Lullaby)

Traditional

This lullaby is a popular Occitan song harmonized and orchestrated by the French musician Joseph Canteloube as part of his collection *Chants d'Auvergne,* composed in the 1920s. Although Canteloube had a close affinity with his region's cultural tradition, he was also a classically trained musician, and his orchestration of the *Chants d'Auvergne* owes much to the music of his teacher, Vincent d'Indy.

The popular character of the lullaby has been restored on the version found on the CD by dispensing with Canteloube's ornaments. The simple melody is supported by a drone in the bassoon.

A drone is one or more sustained notes accompanying a melody, a technique found in many traditional types of music. In bagpipe music, for example, some of the pipes are dedicated to producing a drone.

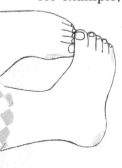

Soun, soun, beni, beni, beni	*Come, slumber, come, come, come*
Soun, soun, beni, beni, doun	*Come, slumber, come, please come*
Lou soun, soun bouol pas beni	*Slumber does not come*
L'efontou s'en bouol pas durmi	*The child will not sleep*

Musical director Sergio Menozzi Explanatory notes Nicolas Tholozan
Illustrations Élodie Nouhen Graphic design Carine Turin and Marc Deroin
for La tête moderne and Stephan Lorti for Haus Design
Translation from French to English for Service d'édition Guy Connolly
Tim Brierly and David Lytle Copy editing Ruth Joseph
Recorded, mixed, edited and mastered by Christophe Germanique

Recorded in the home of Lia and Alexandre Snitkowski at La Verdière
in Bessenay, France. Orchestrations of *The Doll* by Sergio Menozzi
and Naoki Tsurusaki, of *Solveig's Song* and *The Toybox* by Fabrice Pierre

Members of L'Ensemble Agora: Catherine Puertolas (flute, alto flute, piccolo),
Hélène Mourot and Philippe Cairey-Remonay (oboe, oboe d'amore, English
horn), Sandrine Pastor-Cavalier (clarinet, basset-horn), Sergio Menozzi (bass
clarinet), Cédric Laggia (bassoon, contrabassoon), David Pastor (French horn)
and Sophie Bellanger (harp)

Ⓦ www.thesecretmountain.com
ⒸⓅ 2015 The Secret Mountain (Folle Avoine Productions)
ISBN 10: 2-924217-24-5 / ISBN 13: 978-2-924217-24-5